WELCOME TO
PASSPORT TO READING
A beginning reader's ticket to a brand-new world!

Every book in this program is designed to build read-along and read-alone skills, level by level, through engaging and enriching stories. As the reader turns each page, he or she will become more confident with new vocabulary, sight words, and comprehension.

These PASSPORT TO READING levels will help you choose the perfect book for every reader.

READING TOGETHER
Read short words in simple sentence structures together to begin a reader's journey.

READING OUT LOUD
Encourage developing readers to sound out words in more complex stories with simple vocabulary.

READING INDEPENDENTLY
Newly independent readers gain confidence reading more complex sentences with higher word counts.

READY TO READ MORE
Readers prepare for chapter books with fewer illustrations and longer paragraphs.

This book features sight words from the educator-supported Dolch Sight Words List. This encourages the reader to recognize commonly used vocabulary words, increasing reading speed and fluency.

For more information, please visit passporttoreadingbooks.com.

Enjoy the journey!

Little, Brown and Company
Hachette Book Group
1290 Avenue of the Americas, New York, NY 10104
Visit us at LBYR.com

First Edition: October 2017

Little, Brown and Company is a division of Hachette Book Group, Inc.
The Little, Brown name and logo are trademarks of Hachette Book Group, Inc.

The publisher is not responsible for websites
(or their content) that are not owned by the publisher.

Library of Congress Control Number 2017940706

ISBNs: 978-0-316-43612-0 (pbk.), 978-0-316-43614-4 (ebook),
978-0-316-43613-7 (ebook), 978-0-316-43611-3 (ebook)

Printed in the United States of America

CW

10 9 8 7 6 5 4 3 2 1

Passport to Reading titles are leveled by independent reviewers applying the standards
developed by Irene Fountas and Gay Su Pinnell in *Matching Books to Readers:
Using Leveled Books in Guided Reading*, Heinemann, 1999.

Masha and the Bear®

The Best Birthday

Adapted by **Lauren Forte**
From the episode **"Once Upon a Year"**
written by **Oleg Kuzovkov**
art directed by **I. Trusov**

LITTLE, BROWN AND COMPANY
New York   Boston

Featuring Masha

and the Bear!

4

Attention, Masha and the Bear fans!
Look for these words
when you read this book.
Can you spot them all?

gift

snowman

balloon

fireworks

Today is the Bear's birthday.
His friends visit for a party.

"I forgot today is the Bear's birthday,"
says Masha.
"Where can I get a gift?"
Masha has to think fast.

"Happy birthday, Bear!"
Masha shouts.
She made a snowman
for her friend.

"My birthday is very soon,"
Masha says.
"Do not forget."

The next day, Masha says,
"Here are the gifts I want."
The list is long.

Masha's birthday
is months away.
But she is ready!

As the weeks pass,
Masha leaves notes for her friends.
Each note counts down the days.

She writes a lot of notes.
She puts them everywhere.

When her birthday arrives, Masha is excited!

But her friends are not outside. "Where are they?" Masha asks. "Maybe they are waiting for me at the Bear's house."

Masha opens the Bear's door.

"Here I am," she says.

But nobody is there.

"Did they really forget?"
Masha wonders.

Masha looks for her friends.
They are not in the van.

They are not in Squirrel's tree.

Where are they?

The wind catches Masha's balloon.
It pulls her into the air.

POP!

The balloon bursts.

Masha tumbles through the trees.

"This is my worst birthday," she says.

Masha walks home
singing softly to herself.
"Happy birthday to me..."

When she gets home,
lights flash.
Balloons pour out of
the windows.

It is a surprise party!

Masha cannot believe her eyes.

Fireworks go off in the sky.
They are beautiful.

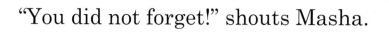

"You did not forget!" shouts Masha.

When she sees her friends,
she feels happy again.

The Bear even gives Masha
a new balloon.

They have cake, and everyone sings.
It is Masha's best birthday ever.

The Bear gives Masha a hug.
Masha does not need presents.
She just needs her friends.